Mutiny!

Sam scrambled onboard, heaving himself up and sliding on to the deck belly-first. He lay silently for a minute, his heart pounding and his knees weak. He was so happy to be safely on the ship that he could have kissed the deck but there was no time for that. *This was mutiny!*

Look out for more
stories of swashbuckling
space adventures in

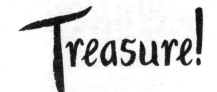

Stowaway!

Stranded!

Treasure!

SPACE  PIRATES

Mutiny!

JIM LADD

Illustrated by
Benji Davies

nosy
crow

With special thanks to Paul Harrison
To the parentals; steering the ship safely through choppy waters

First published in the UK in 2014 by Nosy Crow Ltd,
The Crow's Nest, 10a Lant Street, London SE1 1QR, UK

Nosy Crow and associated logos are trademarks and/or registered
trademarks of Nosy Crow Ltd

Text © Hothouse Fiction, 2014
Illustrations © Benji Davies, 2014

The right of Hothouse Fiction to be identified as the author of this work
has been asserted by them in accordance with the Copyright, Designs and
Patents Act, 1988

1 3 5 7 9 10 8 6 4 2

A CIP catalogue record for this book is available from the British Library

Printed and bound in the UK by Clays Ltd, St Ives Plc

Papers used by Nosy Crow are made from wood grown in sustainable forests.

ISBN: 978 0 85763 228 9

www.nosycrow.com

Who's who in
COMET'S CREW

CAPTAIN COMET

SAM STARBUCK

BARNEY

PEGG AND LEGG

Who's who in
BLACK-HOLE BEARD'S CREW

BAGGOT

YARR

BLACK-HOLE BEARD

Chapter One

CASTAWAY AHOY!

Samson Starbuck peered at the bowl of food in front of him and wrinkled his nose. Breakfast on board pirate spaceship the *Jolly Apollo* was never good, but today's looked *awful*. The bowl contained a thick grey liquid halfway between porridge and soup, which seemed to be both watery *and* lumpy at the same time. It smelled of old fish and engine oil.

As Sam stared at the bowl he was sure that something in it moved. Feeling sick, he pushed the bowl away and sat up. All around him in the mess hall, his fellow crew mates were digging into the disgusting gloop hungrily.

"How can you eat that?" Sam asked Piole, the pirate sitting next to him. "It's revolting!"

Piole turned to look at Sam, food dribbling from three of his twelve mouths.

"The food here is *always* revolting," Piole replied. "But it's the only food we get so you may as well make the most of it. Aren't you eating yours?"

"No, do you want it?" Sam knew the answer

already – Piole would eat just about anything.

"Cheers, me hearty!" said Piole, swapping Sam's bowl for his own empty one.

Sam felt the slap of a large tentacle on his shoulder and turned to see Barney, the ship's cook, standing behind him. Although Barney looked fearsome – he was a gigantic, multi-tentacled Kraken – he was actually Sam's best friend.

"Morning, Sam," said Barney. "Finished already? You must be growing – here, have some more!"

He slopped out another ladleful of the disgusting gloop into the empty bowl before wandering off, whistling a merry space shanty to himself. Sam groaned and leaned his head on the table.

"Growing?" Romero, the huge lobster-clawed snippernaut, guffawed. "Sam could grow for a Traxonion year and he'd still be a space sprat!"

"Hey!" Sam protested as the other pirates laughed.

"Aye, aye, shipmate," said Captain Comet to Sam, plonking himself down on the bench.

Comet was one of the most extravagantly dressed space pirates in the Universe. He liked bright frock coats and always wore a tricorn hat. He had eye patches covering two of his three eyes and a long waxed moustache that stuck out from each side of his face like curled wire.

Comet might look like a perfect pirate, but Sam knew he and his crew were widely regarded as the most useless space pirates in all the known galaxies – and probably the unknown galaxies as well. However, beneath all the bluster, bragging, incompetence and cowardice, Captain Comet had a heart of gold and truly cared for his crew.

Which was just as well, because Sam had joined the *Jolly Apollo* to try and rescue his parents, who had been space-shipwrecked on the mysterious Planet X. The pirates were only too happy to help. The planet was rumoured to be made of solid gold. And Sam had a map of how to get there!

"What's wrong, are you space-sick?" asked Captain Comet.

Sam shook his head.

"So what is it, me hearty? It can't be that bad!"

Sam picked up his bowl. The grey sludge shuddered and a bubble popped at the surface, releasing a smell like the inside of an old bowling shoe.

"Oh," said Comet. "It *is* that bad." He grimaced and pushed the bowl towards Piole, who gave the captain a cheery wink.

"Anyhow," Comet continued, "I thought you'd like a quick status update – we're making good progress. We've passed the Corkscrew Galaxy and I think we should reach this wormhole soon." He pointed to the scrap of spacesuit material on which Sam's mother had drawn the map.

Sam raised his head and looked at it excitedly. They were getting closer by the minute! And they had managed not to get lost for three days now – a *Jolly Apollo* record.

"Castaway ahoy! Castaway ahoy!"

The shout from the crow's nest was loud and clear, even down in the mess hall.

"A-ha, sounds like we've spotted someone," said Comet. "Some poor hapless soul, cast adrift on a barren rock with their meagre possessions. They're lucky we've found them; I've heard of castaways going mad from loneliness, or getting so hungry they've been reduced to eating their own socks."

Sam gulped as he thought about his own parents stranded on the distant Planet X. *But they*

wouldn't have to eat their own socks, Sam thought to himself. *They're both botanists, and they know everything there is to know about planets from all over the galaxy. They'll definitely be able to find food, even on a barren planet that's supposed to be made of gold. Won't they?*

Comet rose from the bench and interrupted Sam's thoughts. "Let's go and see who it is," he said.

Sam trooped up to the main deck with the crew, all eager to catch a glimpse of who it was the lookout had spotted. In the distance they could see someone waving from a large asteroid.

"Set a course for the asteroid please, Mr Pegg and Mr Legg," Comet called to the two-headed first mate who was steering the *Jolly Apollo*. Legg, the happier head, saluted sharply, while Pegg concentrated on the wheel.

The asteroid was small and round, barely big enough for a bowling lane, and piled high with suitcases. The castaway didn't seem too upset about being stranded. Leaning against a

couple of his suitcases, he calmly waved to the approaching ship as if he didn't much care if they stopped or not. Sam frowned as he looked at him. The stowaway didn't look like he was marooned and desperate. He was wearing a gold-coloured cape over some pretty fancy pirate clothes and had a gold peg leg.

As the *Apollo* pulled alongside the stranger he tossed his head, flicking his wild black hair away from his face.

"Ahoy, me hearties!" he shouted in a deep voice. "What took you so long?"

"Ahoy!" called Comet. "Stand back, I'm coming down."

He dropped a rope ladder down to the asteroid and turned to Sam. "Rule fifty-six, paragraph three of the pirate code," he explained. "You always pick up a castaway. Now just watch his face when he realises he's been rescued by the famous Captain Joseph Hercules Invictus Comet!"

Sam held back a laugh. Comet rushed to put

on his formal hat, the one with the extra-large feather, then perched on the side of the spaceship and gave a nonchalant salute to the crew before throwing his feet over the ship's rails. Unfortunately his foot caught on the top rung of the rope ladder and instead of climbing down, he tipped over headfirst, and ended up dangling from the ladder by his feet, swinging over the asteroid.

"Ahhhhhhhhh!" he yelled as he untangled himself and landed in a heap.

The stranger reached down, grabbed Comet by the

scruff of the neck and hauled him to his feet.

Comet's hat was wedged down over his head and he wobbled around the asteroid as he struggled to get it off – much to the castaway's amusement. With one last mighty heave the hat flew off and Comet fell on his backside. The captain sat there blinking his one good eye in befuddlement. The stranger stared with a wry smile at the three-eyed pirate.

"There you go, Patches! Right way up again," said the stranger.

"Ah, erm, thank you," Comet replied, looking a bit flustered. He took a deep breath and puffed out his chest. "I'm Captain Com—"

"Be a good fellow," the stranger interrupted, "and grab those bags for me, will you? Getting up the ship's ladder is going to be a struggle with this."

He motioned to his golden peg leg, then gave Comet a wink and a pat on the cheek. "Make way, boys!" the stranger called up to the *Apollo*. "I'm coming aboard!"

Chapter Two

GOLDSTAR!

The stranger climbed easily up the ladder to the *Jolly Apollo* and vaulted athletically over the rail, landing nimbly on the deck.

"Ahoy there!" he called, his hands on his hips and his chin jutting out proudly.

He breathed in deeply and started to wander about. "Hah, it's good to be back on the deck of a pirate ship again!" he exclaimed, slapping the main mast.

The crew of the *Apollo* watched in open-mouthed amazement as the stranger swaggered around the ship as if he owned it.

"Hi," said Sam. "So, erm, what's your name?"

The stranger spun round, stared at Sam and smiled broadly.

"They call me," he paused dramatically, "Goldstar."

There was a gasp and a thump as Comet struggled over the rails with Goldstar's cases and landed in a heap on the deck.

"Why do they call you that?" asked Barney, completely ignoring the captain and staring at

Goldstar excitedly.

"Who knows?" Goldstar replied with a wicked smile. "It might be because I always wear gold…" he flicked his cape. "It might be because of this…" he tapped his golden peg leg on the deck. "Or it might be because of this!" With a flourish he opened the bag he'd been holding and revealed a solid gold bowling ball.

The crew gasped as one with a sound like a Paloovian snotwhale about to sneeze.

"What?" Sam asked. He knew bowling was every space pirate's favourite sport, but he'd never seen a gold ball before.

"A golden ball!" Barney explained in a hushed whisper. "It's the prize for winning the Interstellar Bowling Championship!"

Goldstar lifted the ball from the bag and turned it so that everyone could see five diamonds glinting on its surface. "Five years in a row," Goldstar grinned at the awed audience. "Eventually they had to ban me so others could have a chance. One of my strikes in the last championship was

voted Shot of the Millennium by the Tri-Galaxy
Federation. They carefully pulled up the bowling
lane and re-installed it in the Hall of Fame."

Everyone looked on in dumbstruck awe. Vulpus
and Piole exchanged amazed glances; Jonjarama,
the gassiest member of the crew, trumped loudly
with excitement; even Pegg, the grumpier head
of the first mate, looked amazed.

Only Comet didn't seem impressed as he bent
against the ship's rail, trying
to catch his breath.

"Now, how about
a glass of grum to
celebrate being
rescued!" said
Goldstar.

Everyone cheered.
Grum, a sort of lemonade
milkshake, was a pirate's favourite
drink. The only thing they enjoyed as
much as bowling was a tankard of
grum and a singsong.

Mutiny!

"Actually," wheezed Comet, "we've got lots of chores to do today to get the old girl space-ship-shape—"

"And if you guys point me in the direction of a bowling lane," said Goldstar, ignoring Comet, "then I can show you how I did that strike."

With another cheer Goldstar was rushed below decks by the crew. Comet and Sam were the only ones left. They stood looking at the empty deck in stunned silence.

"Well," Comet muttered to himself, "I suppose a little glass of grum would be fine, just this once, welcome him aboard and all that…"

"You all right, Captain?" asked Sam.

"What? Yes, yes, absolutely fine. Come on, come on, let's get a move on or all the best lanes will be taken."

Sam followed Captain Comet down to the lower deck where the bowling lanes were. All space pirate ships had at least one bowling lane, but the *Jolly Apollo* had more than most. That was because the *Apollo* used the space that other pirate ships used for storing treasure and laser cannons – two things that Captain Comet's ship didn't really have – for extra bowling lanes. They'd never been successful enough to find any treasure, and they'd managed to lose most of their laser cannons years ago in an unfortunate incident involving Comet and the oozing quicksand of planet Swampiola.

But when Sam and Comet got to the bowling deck no one was bowling; instead everyone was crowded around Goldstar, who was regaling the crew with his stories.

"So that's how I ended up being marooned," said Goldstar as he finished another story. "And I believe Admiral Mercury is still trying to find his telescope – and his trousers!"

The crew burst into laughter and someone raised a toast to Goldstar. Comet sniffed jealously.

"How did you come by that peg leg?" asked Vulpus, the fox-like pirate.

"Ah me old peggler," said Goldstar, looking at the golden stump at the end of his leg. "I lost me leg to a grumigator – he bit it clean off."

"Oooh," Barney sighed.

Sam had had a close encounter with grumigators himself and knew they were big enough and ferocious enough to bite off a leg and a whole lot more.

"Anyhow, the way I saw it," Goldstar continued, "if he was going to have my leg, then I should have something of his in return – so I took these."

He felt inside the neck of his shirt and pulled

out a necklace made of
grumigator teeth. Barney
gasped and Sam had to
admit that they were
the biggest teeth he had
ever seen.

"Turns out that particular
beast had been terrorising the
local village on this particular
planet, so the natives made me
this leg as a thank you for ridding
them of the beast."

Goldstar lifted his golden peg leg to show it

off to them in more detail.

The crew applauded wildly. Comet cleared his throat loudly. Sam looked over at him and smiled. Comet did not like being upstaged by anybody – especially aboard his own ship. Sam wondered what Comet could possibly say that would top that last story.

"Fighting with lake lizards is all well and good for a hobby, I suppose," said Comet, giving a large pretend yawn. "But I'm just too busy for that kind of thing. You see, *I'm* going to be the first pirate to find Planet X!"

Goldstar gave a loud booming laugh, which echoed around the bowling alley and gave him a strike on at least three lanes. He wiped his eyes. "And how, pray tell, are you going to find it, *eh*? What makes you so different from all those other hopeless dreamers who have searched for it before?" he asked.

Suddenly Sam had a horrible idea of what Comet was going to do – surely he wouldn't be so stupid as to show the map to a total stranger, especially after his sworn enemy (and the most fearsome pirate ever known), Captain Black-Hole Beard, had tried to steal it? Only a person of intergalactic idiocy would do that.

"The difference is, I've got a map," said Comet, puffing his chest out proudly.

Sam groaned.

"Ha – a map he says!" barked Goldstar, shaking his head. "By the rings of Jalangar, you're a funny one. As if such a thing existed!"

Don't show him, don't show him, willed Sam. "Er, Captain—" he started, but it was too late.

"It does, I have, and here it is!" said Comet, flashing the map at Goldstar.

Sam slapped his hand on to his forehead in despair. Goldstar grabbed Comet's wrist and peered at the scrap of silver cloth, and his eyes hardened for the briefest of moments. It was only for a flash, but to Sam it seemed as if a mask had slipped, revealing the true Goldstar underneath – and it was not a pretty sight.

"Well Captain, I've got to hand it ye," laughed

Goldstar, "you're a better man than me."

Comet visibly swelled with pride.

"It's a rare thing you have there, me hearties; a map to the greatest treasure hoard in the entire Universe. Unimagined wealth of immeasurable value…" Goldstar leaned back and stroked his gold peg leg thoughtfully. "You are blessed indeed, and possibly even luckier than you imagine. I noticed from that there map of yours that you're going past the Ninth Vector – near a little planet called Bowlopia. I think you'll find it interesting."

"Why's that?" asked Comet, all eager and pleased with himself.

"Why? Because you're pirates! And Bowlopia," Goldstar's voice rose until he was shouting, "BOWLOPIA IS A PIRATE'S PARADISE!"

Chapter Three

BOWLOPIA!

Mutiny!

"Ah, me hearties!" Goldstar cried out, fixing the pirates with a manic glare. "What can I tell you about Bowlopia? It's a strange world; there's only one sport played there…"

The crew looked confused.

"…and that's bowling!" cried Goldstar.

The crew cheered.

"There's only one type of drink on Bowlopia…" said Goldstar.

The crew began to grumble.

"…but that drink is grum!" shouted Goldstar.

The crew cheered again.

"And if you ever want a break from the bowling, there's a gigantic funfair, too!" said Goldstar, his arms spread wide to demonstrate the size.

The crew cheered once more.

"And the best thing is, we're only a day's sail away!" shouted Goldstar.

Everyone was beside themselves with excitement. Jonjarama was so thrilled he did a massive fart but everyone was so caught up with the idea of Bowlopia that no one cared.

"But what about Planet X?" said Sam, struggling to be heard above the noise. "What about rescuing my parents?"

Goldstar gave a smarmy smile and went over to slap Comet on the back like an old friend.

"I'm sure your good captain here would approve," said Goldstar, ignoring Sam. "After all, a leader of his strength, good-looks, wit and experience knows how to let his hair down – he's a proper pirate, so he is."

Comet swelled with pride. "Well, I do think a little bit of rest and relaxation would do us all the world of good. Ain't that right?" he blustered. "Set course for Bowlopia!"

Barney and the others started dancing around the deck singing, "We're going to Bowlopia!" at the top of their voices.

Sam seemed to be the only one who was disappointed. "Oh, don't worry!" Comet told him. "It's only one day off course. We'll be there for a day at most and then we'll get back on track. And who knows, with a fair solar wind we'll

probably actually make up time!"

Goldstar grinned, the occasional gold tooth visible in his wolf-like smile. "They say you've never truly bowled until you've bowled the ring of Bowlopia."

Barney raced over to Sam, a huge smile plastered across his face and a tankard of grum clutched in each of his tentacles.

"Is it just me, Barney, or is there something a bit odd about Goldstar?" Sam asked. "Did you see his face when he looked at the map?"

"He seems pretty cool to me," Barney replied. "And he's taking us to Bowlopia! Here, have a grum – enjoy yourself."

Sam took the grum and watched Goldstar as he wandered around the bowling deck, laughing with the crew, slapping them on the back, shaking hands. Everyone else seemed to love him. But there was something about that wild black hair that bothered Sam... *His hair?* Sam suddenly shook his head, feeling bad. He couldn't decide he didn't like someone because of their hair.

He'd been worrying about his parents too much. Maybe a day at Bowlopia would be just what he needed. Sam took a swig of the grum. Yes, it was definitely time for some fun!

The closer the *Jolly Apollo* got to Bowlopia, the more excited everyone became. By the time Vulpus, the lookout, caught sight of the planet, the ship was buzzing.

Sam raced to look over the side. Bowlopia was a huge blue planet, with three dark patches on the surface like the finger-holes in a bowling ball. Around it looped a shimmering golden circle.

"See the ring around the planet, me hearties?" asked Goldstar. "That's a giant bowling lane, the longest one in the universe! Your ball goes all the way around the planet!"

Sam felt his mouth drop open in amazement. All around him everyone else was

staring open-mouthed as well.
Piole's twelve mouths
were making a
puddle of drool
on the deck.

"Before we get to the bowling, what say you we have a go on the funfair first?" said Goldstar.

"That has to be some funfair to beat bowling around a planet," said Pegg sceptically.

"Oh, but it is – look!" said Goldstar, as the largest funfair any of them had ever seen in their lives came into view.

"It must be the size of a city," said Legg, the other head of the first mate.

"Well, what are we waiting for?" Comet said grandly. "Prepare to land!"

"I'll fly us!" said Pegg.

"No – I will!" Legg wrestled the steering wheel away from him.

"I will!" Pegg growled.

While Pegg and Legg launched into one of their usual arguments, the *Jolly Apollo* was heading full speed towards the planet.

"I like a crew that's keen!" Goldstar chuckled nervously. "But should we be slowing down?"

"I'm sure they'll stop eventually," said Comet. "They usually do."

"Erm, we are getting a bit close," Sam said anxiously.

"Reverse thrusters!" Comet yelled.

Pegg and Legg jumped, and turned to see a huge neon sign rushing towards them. It was an enormous picture of a bowling ball and ten hoverpins, with *WELCOME TO BOWLOPIA!* written across it.

They flipped on the thrusters, and the *Jolly Apollo* creaked and groaned under the strain as the engines tried to pull the rusting hull in the opposite direction to the one it was travelling in.

Sam grabbed the ship's wheel and turned it sharply. The ship lurched to one side, but it was still travelling too fast.

"Batten the hatches!" shouted Comet, diving for cover. "She's going to crash!"

With a horrible wailing of engines, the *Jolly Apollo* ploughed side-on into the massive sign. Huge hoverpins pinged off everywhere as the *Apollo* ground to a halt. Finally it stopped on top of the flattened sign, lying at a funny angle on mangled metal, thin wisps of smoke coming from the thrusters.

"Now that's what I call a strike!" shouted Goldstar, roaring with laughter.

Sam was still clinging on to the wheel, his knuckles white from holding on so tightly. Close by he saw Comet peering from his hiding place inside an empty grum barrel.

The captain patted himself over to feel for any injuries, and satisfied all was well, clambered on to the listing deck. He nodded with approval. "Well, I've had worse landings, I must admit. Nice work, Sam," he said.

"Don't mention it,"
Sam smiled.

Pegg and Legg started arguing about
whose fault it was, but Goldstar interrupted
grandly. "Look at it, me hearties!" he crowed.
"Like I told you, pirate paradise!"

The crew looked on in wide-eyed amazement.
All around them were the twisting tracks of
the hovercoasters, whirling antigravity rides,
bright coloured lights and pirates from all over
the seven solar seas. The competing sounds of
music playing from different rides filled the air,
along with the sound of the crowds cheering
and screaming, and stall holders crying out their

wares. The air smelt of supernova floss, hot Wumpfle dogs and grum.

"Come on then, lads," shouted Goldstar, "it's fun time! Follow me and I won't let you down!"

"Captain, we're only going to spend *one* day here, aren't we? My parents still need rescuing…" said Sam, but Comet was already half way down the gangplank, following in Goldstar's wake.

"What was that? Parents? Yes, yes, whatever…" he called back, not bothering to look at Sam.

Sam wasn't convinced, but before he could complain Barney grabbed him by the arm, pulling him along.

"Come on, Sam, don't worry so much. We'll be back on the search for Planet X before you know it. Last one to the antigravity dodgems is a loser!"

Chapter Four

BOWLING BATTLE

Sam woke up as the movement of the ship made his hover-hammock swing. "Bleurgh!" he groaned, grabbing his stomach. He'd eaten far too much supernova floss yesterday. They had stayed at the funfair all day and most of the night. Sam glanced around at the rest of the hammocks in the crew's sleeping quarters. Vulpus' fur was still plastered back from riding the comet coaster so many times, Zlit's hammock was stuffed with toys he had won on the laser-blaster ranges, and there was a faint moaning from Piole's hammock. He sounded as sick as Sam felt.

Sam dragged himself out of his hammock.

Mutiny!

They had to get going.

"Rise and shine," he said, trying to sound cheerful. "If we get started soon we'll be able to catch up on the time we lost yesterday."

The response was a grumbling from the hammocks.

Just then Goldstar burst into the room with Captain Comet staggering behind him. Goldstar looked no worse the wear for a night of supernova floss and grum. His eyes flashed, his gold teeth glinted and his cape shimmered in the light.

Comet, however, looked like he'd been dragged though a wormhole backwards.

"Yo ho ho, me hearties!" Goldstar boomed. "What say you we take a turn bowling round the planetary ring?"

The crew cheered and Sam's stomach fell. They'd never turn down a day's bowling. To his relief Captain Comet spoke up.

"Sorry, Goldstar, but I made a pledge to Sam that we'd set sail today for Planet X. A pirate's word is his bond, you…"

"Yadda, yadda, yadda," Goldstar said, waving his hand in front of his mouth like he was yawning. "What's wrong, Comet? Think the bowling will be too tough for ye?"

Comet bristled at the insult; his moustache twitched, his face turned red and his eyebrows beetled. Sam groaned, but not with sickness this time. He knew his captain could never turn down a challenge.

"I'll have you know," Comet said in a strained voice, "that I'm an *excellent* bowler – in fact I hold the *Apollo* record for the most points scored in a game – it's just I said to Sam..."

"Oh, a star bowler are ye?" said Goldstar. "Then perhaps you and me ought to have a little competition?"

All the crew cheered; they loved a good bowling contest.

"Don't do this!" Sam hissed at Comet. "He's trying to wind you up. Think about how impressed the other pirates are going to be when *you're* the one who discovers Planet X..."

"Yes, yes, quite right." Comet raised himself to his full height and tried to look as noble as possible while trying to ignore Goldstar's taunt.

"This isn't the time for competitions," he muttered. "After all, we are on an important mission..."

"Not turning a bit Pangolian *chicken* on me, are you, Comet?" Goldstar mocked, giving the crew a conspiratorial wink as he flapped his arms like wings. They chuckled. Comet's face turned even redder and he started huffing and puffing like

he was trying to blow out a fire on the end of his nose. Sam slapped his hand on his face in despair – he knew what was going to happen next.

"Surely," Goldstar continued, "all those stories they tell in the grum bars in the pirate ports about 'Cowardly Comet' can't be true, can they? Not scared of a little bowling game, are you, Captain?"

"Of course I'm not! I'll beat you any time, any lane!" Comet exploded.

"Excellent – that's settled then!" Goldstar smiled. "Let's hit the bowling ring right now!"

"Hooray!" Barney waved his tentacles in the air excitedly. "Let's bowl!"

Mutiny!

One by one the pirates rolled out of their hover hammocks and followed a grinning Goldstar and a bemused-looking Comet to catch a grav-lift out to the planet's ring.

Sam shook his head as he followed the others. Trust Comet to fall for Goldstar's quick talking. All he could do now was follow the rest and try to get them back on board the *Apollo* as soon as possible after the game.

As he got off the grav-lift, Sam couldn't help but be amazed by the view. The ring was a thick golden strip that disappeared into the distance as it stretched right around the planet. Sam looked over the edge and his knees went weak. The only thing he could make out on the planet below were the flashing lights of the gigantic funfair.

All around them was deep, dark space. Ahead lay the biggest bowling lane Sam had ever seen in his life. He watched as a nearby pirate released a ball out on to the ring. The ball disappeared at great speed and a short while later had sped right round the planet and smashed into the hovering pins behind him.

"Shall I start?" said Goldstar, heaving his golden bowling ball out of its bag. It was so shiny that Sam could see the reflection of Comet's worried-looking face in it – perhaps he had forgotten how good a bowler Goldstar was.

Sam watched as Goldstar brought his arm back and fired off his bowling ball. The ball disappeared at lightning pace down the lane and was soon lost from sight. Sam turned round to look at the pins behind him – just as Goldstar's ball sped around the planet. With a clatter all ten pins were scattered across the lane – strike! Goldstar flashed Comet a confident, gold-toothed smile before bowing to the cheering crowd. Sam sighed. He had been hoping that Goldstar had been lying about being a bowling champion and that Comet would win. Goldstar might be a smug idiot, but he was *really* good at bowling.

Eventually, with a clatter of pins, Goldstar got his last strike and won the game by a mile. Even all Comet's cheating hadn't been enough to beat him. Comet had tried every trick in the book – as well as some he'd made up on the spot, like trying to replace Goldstar's bowling ball with a moon rock when he wasn't looking – but it was hopeless. Goldstar got a strike every single time – even with the rock.

Once, Goldstar had flung his ball straight up in the air and Sam had been pleased, thinking that the pirate had finally made a mistake. Comet had hopped up and down excitedly – but then there was a strange whistling sound behind them and the ball boomeranged around the planet and smashed back down, knocking all the pins over. Comet had looked like he was about to cry. Distracted and upset, his next ball had flown right off the ring, missing all the pins, and kept on going, floating out into space.

As the *Apollo*'s crew mobbed Goldstar, Comet looked utterly miserable.

"Three cheers for Goldstar!" Romero bellowed, lifting the smug castaway on to his shoulders. "Hip, hip, hooray! Hip, hip, hooray! Hip, hip, hooray!"

As the pirates carried Goldstar off, Sam tried to console Comet. "Don't worry, Captain; he *is* an intergalactic champion after all."

"I don't mind losing," Comet replied.

Sam raised his eyebrows.

"OK, I *do*," Comet admitted, "but what makes it worse is all of *that*!"

He looked at Goldstar laughing and joking with the crew as they headed back to the ship. Comet and Sam trudged the rest of the way behind them in silence.

No sooner had they got on deck than Goldstar yawned extravagantly.

"Well, I think I'll go for a little nap. You don't mind if I take your cabin, do you, Patches?"

Without waiting for an answer he marched into Comet's cabin and shut the door. Captain Comet stood opened-mouthed, then, realising the crew were watching him, tried to laugh it off.

"Yes, yes, of course," he called, "just like we agreed earlier..." Comet was trying his best to sound convincing.

Sam looked at his captain. "I reckon he's up to something," he said.

Comet nodded vigorously. "Aye, me heartie," he said. "I've always thought there was something strange about him."

Sam rolled his eyes. Comet was only suspicious now Goldstar had beaten him at bowling!

"Pity there's no way of spying on him," said Sam.

"Oh, but there is, me hearty," said Comet, with a wicked smile. "I'll show you."

He took a quick look about and cleared his throat.

"Ah, Sam," he said, just loud enough for other people to hear. "I, er, require your assistance to check the hold – make sure we've got enough grum and all that."

"Aye, aye, Captain," Sam replied and followed Comet down to the dark, dingy room at the back of the boat where they kept all the grum.

"There's a secret passage from here to my cabin," Comet explained. "It's handy if I ever get

thirsty in the middle of the night."

"But the grum store is meant to be triple locked – no one is allowed in here by themselves!" said Sam.

Comet froze for a moment. "Erm, did I say 'thirsty'?" he stammered. "I meant to say 'worried'. You know, that someone was breaking in to, er, steal some. Slip of the grum – I mean tongue. Yes. Slip of the, er, tongue. Anyway, shall we get on?"

Without waiting for an answer, Comet went over to a barrel in the far corner of the room and popped off the top. Then he climbed inside and disappeared. Sam peered in and saw that inside the barrel was a hole, just big enough for Comet to squeeze through. He clambered inside and followed. There was a narrow tunnel ahead of him, mainly filled with Comet's disappearing bottom. Sam crept forwards until he reached the captain. Above him was a trapdoor, which Comet carefully prised open a notch. A slither of light illuminated his face and the sound of Goldstar's voice filled the tunnel. Sam squatted below the captain, looking up.

"What's going on?" Sam asked.

"I don't believe it!" Comet hissed as he peered into the room.

"What?" Sam asked in a whisper.

"He's got his muddy boot on my pillow," Comet grumbled. "And he's wearing my dressing gown.

And he's got my ceremonial wig on!" Comet was outraged. "That's for captains, that is!"

"But what's *happening*?" Sam asked again.

"He's talking to someone on my holoscreen," said Comet. "Here, have a look."

Sam tried squeezing alongside and for an uncomfortable moment got his face wedged in Comet's armpit. Eventually he managed to catch a glimpse into the cabin. He could see Goldstar's boot and peg-leg propped up as he lay stretched out on Comet's bed.

"I reckons you're right, big brother," Goldstar replied. There was a laugh from the holoscreen.

Sam thought there was something familiar about that laugh. He was sure he'd heard it somewhere before. It was a horrible, cruel kind of a sound.

"Who's he talking to?" asked Sam.

"I don't know, I can't see the screen," Comet hissed in reply, "but I don't think it's good – my moustache is starting to twitch."

Sam cautiously pushed the wooden trapdoor

a little higher. A familiar face filled the huge holoscreen.

It was a great bearded pirate, with a foul beast, half-spacerat, half-parrot, perched on his shoulder. Behind him stood a tattooed, one-horned Minocerous.

The Minocerous was huge. He wore a scary-looking necklace made from the bones of some poor creature, an open waistcoat over his bare chest and he was carrying a large, gleaming cutlass.

Comet gasped loudly, and Goldstar turned. Sam quickly dropped the trapdoor.

"Was that…?" Comet whispered.

"Yes!" Sam nodded. "Goldstar was talking to…"

"Black-Hole Beard and his evil first mate, Yarr!" they said together.

Chapter Six

BAD BROTHERS

Sam and Comet crawled backwards as fast as they could until they were back at the grum store. Suddenly everything became clear to Sam.

"I knew there was something about his hair – it's exactly the same as Black-Hole Beard's beard!" he said.

"I can't believe it," muttered Comet. "Goldstar is Black-Hole Beard's little brother! You were right about him all along. That slimy star-swindler! That galaxy gnuggleshooter! Well, we'll teach him to mess with the *Jolly Apollo*!"

"Wait—" Sam interrupted as a plan started to form in his head. "Let's wait and find out what he's up to first, then we can work out how to stop him."

Just then, the dinner gong sounded, making both of them jump.

"OK then," Comet sighed. "But then we'll get that no-good, dirty, planet-robbing…" Comet trailed off, muttering under his breath.

As they reached the mess hall, Goldstar strolled in behind them.

"And he wore my wig!" spluttered Comet indignantly. "To think that a relative of Black-Hole Beard has had his great fat head in my ceremonial—"

"Shush – we can't let him know we know, remember," said Sam, under his breath.

Goldstar went to sit down in Comet's chair, just as the captain was sitting down at the same time.

"Oops! Easy there, me hearty – didn't see you," said Goldstar. "Didn't think this seat was taken."

"Oh, no problem," said Comet. "It's just this is the captain's chair…"

Goldstar smiled a thin little smile. "Then of course, Captain, please take your seat."

"No, no, you're the guest, please, you have it," Comet replied, ushering Goldstar to the chair.

"On the contrary, ye should have it," said Goldstar, stepping back.

"No you," said Comet.

"No *ye*," Goldstar replied.

"Well, I suppose I am the captain," said Comet and slipped into his seat and sat down.

Mutiny!

"Yess, ye are, aren't ye..." Goldstar smiled his wolfish smile once more. "Anyway, Cap'n, I was thinking," he said, as he loomed over Comet. "Perhaps this afternoon the crew would like to see the bowling-ball factory next to the grum warehouse?"

Comet looked at Goldstar as he continued. "They could get themselves a custom-made ball and have a drink of grum; thought they might enjoy it. Just an idea…"

Goldstar smiled at Comet again and went to find a seat at one of the tables.

"Actually, that does sound like fun," whispered Comet to Sam.

"Have you forgotten who we're dealing with?" Sam replied in exasperation.

"Oh, yes, sorry," said Comet.

"I think he's trying to keep us here for some reason," Sam said thoughtfully. "It must have something to do with Black-Hole Beard."

"Well, in that case, we need to get going," Comet said firmly. "Time for a captain's announcement!"

Captain Comet stood up and tapped his knife against his metal tankard to get everyone's attention.

Mutiny!

The noise in the busy dining hall faded away.

"Good evening and sorry for disturbing your meal – and thank you once again to Barney for his efforts," said Comet.

Goldstar mumbled something to the pirates sitting next to him, who laughed.

Comet gave them a hard stare and continued. "Well, I hope you've all enjoyed our visit. I must say, even a seasoned old space dog like myself has never clapped eyes on a planet such as this. Clearly the atmosphere takes a bit of getting used to and it can have a strange effect on your bowling technique…"

Goldstar muttered something again, to much bigger laughs this time.

"…but it is still a fantastic place for a pirate to spend some time. Unfortunately the time has come to leave…"

On the word "leave" there was a chorus of complaints.

"But Captain, there's so much more to see!" said Goldstar.

"Well, yes, I'm sure there is. But we're on a mission to Planet X don't forget—"

"But we want to stay!" Goldstar stood up and raised his arms wide, appealing to the crew. "What say you, me hearties?" he asked the pirates.

There was an uproar of voices all shouting to be heard.

Captain Comet looked shocked. His face began to go red and his moustache started quivering like a franpod jelly. He stood up to his full height and bellowed at the top of his voice, "SILENCE!"

The room went quiet.

"It is not up to the crew," said Comet, clearly and deliberately, "and it's not up to you, Goldstar. *I* decide where and when the *Jolly Apollo* sails, because *I* am the captain!"

It was so quiet that you could hear the rust flaking off the ship's hull.

"Except," said Goldstar, a slow, sly, smile stretching across his face, "if a captain goes against the wishes of his hearty crew, perhaps he shouldn't be captain any more…"

Chapter Seven

MUTINY!

Captain Comet's face turned white.

"This is mutiny," he whispered, as if he couldn't quite believe what was happening.

Goldstar leaped from his seat.

"What do ye say, me hearties? Is this what you want? Scuttling about the galaxies on this old rust bucket? Working all day and then hanging in hammocks at night?"

Pegg yelled out, "No!" Legg's usual cheeriness wavered. The crew looked unsure.

"Why do all that," Goldstar continued, "when you could be having a bit of hard-earned, well-deserved rest here?"

More of the crew muttered in agreement and the cheers grew louder. Captain Comet was beginning to look like a Haroonian Jack Rabbit caught in the headlights of a dust racer.

"But we're going to Planet X," Sam insisted. "To find treasure!" His words were lost as Goldstar picked up his bowl and smashed it on to the floor.

"And you call this food?" Goldstar bellowed.

"I thought you'd been draining the hull's toilets. This isn't food fit for proper space pirates!"

Sam looked over at Barney, who seemed to be on the verge of tears. But Goldstar had also seen him.

"Barney, Barney, Barney," he said, patting one of the Kracken's tentacles. "This isn't anything personal. I'm thinking about you. After a hard day aboard the ship, surely you deserve a break too. Look, have some of this."

Goldstar went to a large trunk in the mess room and flung it open. Inside it was filled to the top with supernova floss.

"Here, Barney, you should have the first piece. Now, doesn't that taste good? And you didn't even have to do anything! There's plenty here for everyone – we *are* on Bowlopia after all."

Sam watched as the crew jostled and shoved each other to get at the supernova floss. It was not a dignified sight.

"I tell you, boys, if it were up to me we'd be having supernova floss and grum every day," said

Goldstar, taking a large bite of his sugary treat. "I'd make a *much* better captain than old Patches here," said Goldstar, that evil smile flashing across his face again.

To Sam's horror, there were some mutterings of support from the crew.

"Your problem, Comet, is that you can't see the truth of it even though it's right there in front of you. Too many eyepatches, I reckon."

There was a ripple of laughter.

Sam stood up suddenly.

"Stop it all of you!" he shouted. "Yeah, Goldstar seems like good fun, but you won't be laughing when you find out who he really is."

The smile froze on Goldstar's face and he shot Sam a hard look.

"Goldstar is Black-Hole Beard's brother!" shouted Sam, poking his finger into Goldstar's middle. "You can't trust him as far as you could bowl him!"

There was a loud intake of breath from the crew and they all looked at Goldstar. Goldstar stared back at them. For a second his lower lip wobbled, and Sam thought he was about to burst into tears. Then he started laughing.

"I think the anti-grav rides have affected someone's brains," he said, wiping an imaginary tear from his eye. "In my day I would have been flogged for telling tall tales like that, but thankfully we live in happier times. And, after all, he's just a stowaway isn't he, me hearties?"

A few of the crew murmured their agreement.

Goldstar continued. "Now, what's this buffoonery? Me, Black-Hole Beard's brother? Really? Do I look anything like that old rogue? I don't even have a beard!"

"That's true," Legg muttered.

"And if I was Black-Hole Beard's brother, would I be giving you these?"

Goldstar spread his hands like a magician, revealing a host of tickets.

"Free day-passes for the funfair for everyone!" he crowed.

There were "oohs" and "ahhs" from the crew.

"And not only that – they're *golden* tickets.

Mutiny!

These beauties mean you can jump any queue you see."

The crew cheered.

"I'll tell you again, me hearties, if *I* were captain this is what it would be like all the time: supernova floss, grum and Bowlopia."

The crew cheered again.

"What say you all we put it to the vote?" said Goldstar.

"Vote, vote, vote," chanted the crew.

"What?" Sam stared around at his friends in dismay.

Pegg and Legg shrugged.

"Supernova floss," Legg told Sam sheepishly.

"He's right about the food," Pegg muttered grumpily.

"But you can't just call a vote and decide who's going to be captain!" said Sam, confused and outraged in equal measure.

"Erm, I'm afraid, *technically speaking*, he can," said Comet, his moustache drooping.

"It's the pirate code," Goldstar smirked. "Once

a captain has been in charge for three voyages anyone can challenge him to a vote. If the challenger gets all of the crew's votes, then they become the new captain."

"And how many voyages have you been the captain for?" Sam asked Comet, desperately.

"Ooh, let's see; well, at a rough guess I'd say…" Comet started to count on his ringed fingers.

"Come on…" Goldstar said.

"Hmm, I'm not sure. Less than the stars in the Caslovian galaxy, but more than the warts on a snaffleflax's nose…"

"Captain!" Sam interrupted.

"OK, two…" Comet started.

"Two? But that's fantastic!" Sam yelled.

"…thousand three hundred and fifty-seven," Comet finished sadly.

"Oh. That's a bit more than three," said Sam.

"Indeed," Comet agreed, his moustache drooping miserably.

"Well then, Comet, we both know how this works," said Goldstar.

Mutiny!

Comet nodded and gave a signal. Two buckets were put on the table in front of him and Goldstar. Then Pegg and Legg went into Comet's cabin and came out holding a small, dusty chest.

Barney leaned over to Sam. "Every ship comes with its own captain's chest," he explained.

With great ceremony, and not too much pushing and shoving, Pegg and Legg paraded the chest past the crew, placed it on the table between the buckets, and flicked it open, revealing lots of brass tokens, like old-fashioned coins.

"One coin, one vote," Barney whispered.

Each coin had a skull and crossed laser blasters on one side, and on the other a picture of the *Jolly Apollo*. Pegg threw the coins into the crowd and they arced through the air and bounced off the wooden floorboards. The pirates scrambled to pick up one each, but Sam was left

empty-handed. He dived to snatch up the last one, then watched as it tumbled towards the edge of the deck and floated off into space.

"I didn't get one!" Sam protested.

"What a shame, stowaway," Goldstar hissed. "No coin, no vote."

The crew lined up and shuffled past the two men, dropping their tokens into the bucket placed in front of the person they wanted to vote for. Sam watched in horror as token after token clattered into Goldstar's bucket.

Comet sat with his head in his hands, unable to look at what was happening. Goldstar, however, perched on the edge of the table, beaming and nodding, and handing out funfair passes to everyone as they passed.

Sam couldn't believe that the crew was being duped so easily by Goldstar. They seemed to have turned their backs on Captain Comet just for some sweets and fairground rides. Surely not everyone would fall for it? Then Barney walked up and dropped his token into Goldstar's bucket.

Mutiny!

Sam was gobsmacked.

"Et tu, Barney?" said Comet sadly.

"No, I only ate one," said Barney, looking confused and holding up his empty supernova floss stick.

Comet lapsed back into silence as the last pirate stepped forward and clattered his coin into Goldstar's bucket.

"That's it!" Goldstar shouted triumphantly. "The votes are cast – and the result is unanimous!"

There was a loud cheer from the crew.

"Wait!" Sam started. "I haven't…"

"Move it, worm-breath!" Goldstar snarled, shoving Sam out of his path.

Comet sagged in his seat for a moment then, pulling together what was left of his dignity, sat up straight, took off his hat and handed it to Sam.

"Please pass this to Goldstar, Sam," said Comet. "He's captain now."

67

Chapter Eight
CAPTAIN GOLDSTAR

Sam looked at the captain's hat in his hand then stared up at Goldstar, who was still perched on the edge of the table, smiling smugly.

"Come on then, lad, hand it over," said Goldstar.

"You don't deserve to wear this hat!" shouted Sam. "And you lot should be ashamed of yourselves."

He flung the hat at Goldstar's feet. Goldstar glared at Sam, his black eyes filled with menace.

"You'll pay for your insolence, my lad, you mark my words," he hissed.

The pirate bent over and retrieved the hat from the floor. With a flick of his hand he brushed some dust in Sam's direction, then placed the hat on his head grandly, as if he were a king being crowned. He wandered over to where a large copper cooking pot hung from the ceiling and admired his reflection in its shining polished surface.

"Right then, me hearties, down to business," said Goldstar. "You there, relieve your old captain of that map he's so keen on."

Romero walked uneasily up to Comet, who handed over the map with a resigned air.

"No!" shouted Sam. "That's mine! I need it to find my parents!"

"First mate – restrain that impudent pup!" barked Goldstar.

Two firm hands grabbed Sam's arms.

"Pegg! Legg!" Sam yelled as he struggled.

"Orders are orders," Pegg replied.

"But we're really sorry," added Legg.

Goldstar sauntered over, took the map, then leaned down to stare at Sam. He was so close that Sam could feel his breath on his face.

"You need to quit your yapping, my boy," Goldstar snarled. "This is my map now and there's nothing you can do about it."

Goldstar turned to the crew.

"Right, me hearties, turn on the holoscreen," Goldstar commanded. "I've got a surprise for you all!"

Goldstar grinned broadly as he assembled the crew in front of the giant holoscreen.

"I wonder if it's more news about Bowlopia," said Zlit.

"I bet it's a visit to the grum factory!" Barney jumped up and down.

"No, it'll be the supernova floss mines," Romero guessed.

Sam was still held firmly in Pegg and Legg's clutches. Beside him stood Comet, who somehow looked smaller and more pathetic than usual. All of his usual swagger and bravado had gone, as though it had been stripped away when he'd handed over his hat. Even his moustache drooped sadly.

Goldstar stamped his peg leg on the deck to get everyone's attention. "Well me hearties, many thanks from the bottom of this old sea dog's shrivelled black heart. I knew you'd all see sense about who to make captain, and you didn't let me down."

The crew of the *Apollo* all smiled at each other; all except Sam and Comet.

"Now, I run a tight ship," Goldstar declared.

"So there are going to be some changes around here. The first thing is that we're going to join forces with another vessel. The other ship's captain will be the admiral in charge of our little fleet."

Goldstar flashed his gold-toothed smile at the bemused crew and switched on the holoscreen. The large screen flickered into life and the crew gasped in unison.

"Say hello to *Admiral* Black-Hole Beard!" Goldstar laughed. Black-Hole Beard's face filled the screen: dark eyes burning beneath wild black hair; a long scar disappearing into a curly black beard; gold teeth glinting as he threw back his head and laughed.

"Ahoy there, little brother, a good day's work. Well done!" laughed the fearsome pirate captain. "And who is that I see at the back? Is it Ex-Captain *Vomit*? Back where you belong, Joseph, being a nobody."

Baggot, perched as always on Black-Hole Beard's shoulder, fluffed up its tatty feathers and began to sing:

"There once was a useless Comet,
Who was the worst pirate of all.
He lost the vote,
So he lost his boat!
The captain has taken a fall.
Cawwwrrrrr!"

On the screen, Yarr threw back his head and gave a barking laugh. "Yarrr, arr, arr."

"And as for the rest of you sorry planet-lubbers,"

snarled Black-Hole Beard, "you're going to realise what it's like to be proper pirates instead of the intergalactic imbeciles you are at the moment. My brother here will soon whip you into shape and woe betide anyone who doesn't come up to scratch!" Black-Hole Beard turned to his brother, who promptly saluted.

"Cap'n Goldstar!" Black-Hole Beard gave a wicked smile. "The *Gravity's Revenge* is three days' sail away. I trust you can keep this pathetic excuse for a crew busy until I arrive."

"Aye, aye, Admiral." Goldstar grinned.

Abruptly the screen switched off and the *Apollo* was swept by a wave of stunned silence.

"Right then, you scurvy dogs, you heard your Admiral, let's get this rust bucket of a ship ready to sail!" shouted Goldstar.

"But what about Bowlopia?" cried Barney. "We've got free passes!"

"You might want to check the date on those," said Goldstar, with an evil grin.

Barney put the ticket up to his eyes and read

the small print. "They've expired!" he howled. "That's not fair! I want Captain Comet back!"

"Tough luck, Tentacles, you voted for me and now you're stuck with me for at least three voyages, it's the pirate code," Goldstar snapped. "And as for the passes, there's no time for funfairs now anyway, there's piratin' to do!"

There were outraged grumbles from the crew.

"Silence, you bilge rats!" Goldstar bellowed. "Any complaints and I'll tie you upside down on the yard arm until your toes goes blue and your tentacles fall out! Now you," he poked Pegg and Legg in the chest. "Take that insolent young whelp down to the prison cells. Tentacles – you take your beloved ex-captain."

Nobody moved.

"By Jupiter's moons, do it NOW!" Goldstar boomed, flecks of spit flying out of his mouth. "Or I'll keelhaul the lot of you!"

"Sorry, Goldst— I mean, *Captain* Goldstar, sir," said Barney nervously, "but we don't actually have any prison cells on the ship."

Mutiny!

"A pirate ship without cells? What kind of vessel is this?" snapped Goldstar. "Well, lock them on the bowling deck and we'll deal with them when we meet up with *Gravity's Revenge*."

"Sorry," Pegg and Legg muttered as they grabbed hold of Sam. Barney went as pale as a Quarlodian cuttlefish as he came over to Comet.

"Take 'em away!" Goldstar boomed.

"Sorry," Legg said sadly as he and Pegg hauled Sam and Comet downstairs and pushed them into the bowling alley. The door slammed shut and Sam and Comet found themselves alone, prisoners on their own ship.

Chapter Nine
PRISONERS

Sam raced over to the door. It had been broken when Comet had cheated spectacularly in a bowling match and Romero had wrenched the handle off in frustration. Ever since then, the door had been wedged open by a hoverpin. With that gone and the door slammed shut, there was no way to open it from the inside. *It makes the perfect prison*, Sam thought miserably.

For a while neither of them spoke. Sam sighed as he thought about the way the last few days had gone. They had been getting so close to rescuing his parents, but now they seemed as far away as ever. For a moment he pictured himself at home with his mum and dad and felt a small tear pricking the corner of his eye. He sniffed and shook his head. He *had* to find a way out of this mess and crying about it wasn't going to help.

"Captain, we need an escape plan," said Sam. "The vote wasn't even fair!"

"I'm not captain any more," said Comet sulkily. "See, no hat."

"But your crew need you!" said Sam.

"Those back-stabbing, scurvy dogs!" Comet furiously threw a bowling ball down the track and they both ducked as hoverpins flew everywhere. "They deserve everything they get! I was their captain for two thousand three hundred and fifty-seven voyages! It's like they forgot all those good times we had – like when we…"

Comet paused and frowned.

"…I'm sure there were some good times. And we got all that treasure from, from, erm … I'm *sure* we got some once … anyway, it doesn't matter. What they did was despicable!"

Sam sighed; if he was going to get Comet to help he was going to need a better tactic.

"As we're down here, do you fancy a game?" Sam asked, picking up a bowling ball.

"Might as well," Comet huffed.

They bowled in silence. Sam was trying hard to think up a plan and Comet was still sulking. He didn't even perk up when Sam let him win. In fact he didn't even seem to notice. Suddenly the door to the bowling deck burst open, and Barney

pushed Pegg and Legg inside.

"Ow, that hurt," whined Legg.

"Get your tentacles off me, you great galumphing galoot!" shouted Pegg.

The door slammed shut.

"What are you doing here?" asked Sam.

"We resigned," replied Pegg.

"Resigned?" said Sam.

"Well, we were fired," Legg added honestly. "Goldstar's as bad as his brother, so we refused to work for him."

"And now we've been locked up with you," said Pegg.

"We need to do something about that Goldstar," Pegg and Legg said in unison.

Pegg and Legg rarely agreed about anything, so Sam knew that this was a good sign. Having the first mate back on their side was a start.

The door opened suddenly and Vulpus, the fox-like crew member, was thrown into the makeshift jail.

"What happened to you?" asked Sam, surprised

to see their prison filling up so quickly.

"Apparently I wasn't hauling the sails properly," Vulpus replied.

"He threw you in here for that?" asked Legg. "If he starts locking people up for things like that, there'll be no one left!"

Legg was right. Over the next few hours more and more pirates were thrown into the bowling alley. Every few minutes the door would be opened and another pirate would be pushed inside. Eventually most of the *Apollo*'s crew were imprisoned down below. Sam began to get an idea of what to do.

"Listen everybody, most of the crew are here now," he said.

Mutiny!

"You're telling me," said Jonjarama, the latest pirate to have been jailed. "There's only Barney left up there with Goldstar."

"If Barney opens the door we have to convince him to let us out," said Sam.

"Can't we just hit him?" said Pegg.

"No we can't, we've had enough of this crew turning against each other – we need to work as a team!" said Sam.

"If we can get out of here, we can try and get control of the ship back."

A clanking sound came from the door as it squeaked open.

"I've been sent to jail, too," said Barney standing in the doorway. "But because there's no one else left – I've got to throw myself in! Can you believe it? Get in, you scurvy dog!" he shouted, pushing himself in the back with two of his tentacles.

"Barney! Don't shut the door!" shouted Sam.

"Why?" said the Kraken, as the door slammed behind him. "It wouldn't be much of a prison with an open door, would it?"

"Barney!" groaned the crew.

"What?" Barney said, his tentacles drooping dejectedly as the other pirates glared at him.

"We could have escaped and tried to get rid of Goldstar," explained Sam.

"Oh," said Barney. "Sorry. Getting rid of him would have been good. He was really mean about my food, and he said my tentacles were

leaving sucker marks on everything!"

"Don't worry, Barney," Sam said, his mind whirring. "We'll find another way to get out."

"Yes, but if we're all down here, who's flying the ship?" said Legg.

"If that Goldstar reckons he can do it by himself he's in for a surprise," snarled Pegg. "The kind of surprise that ends with a big crash!"

Chapter Ten

A DARING CLIMB

With a sudden clatter of bowling pins the *Jolly Apollo* lurched violently to one side, scattering pirates everywhere. The ship then tipped the other way, rolling everyone towards one wall and into a big space-piratey pile.

"Ouch! Goldstar's losing control!" cried Comet as a bowling ball bounced off his head.

The ship shook and rattled then leaned over again, causing everyone to slide the other way and the ball to bounce off Comet's head again.

"Will someone please grab hold of that blasted ball!" shouted Comet.

"He'll wreck the ship if he keeps doing this," said Pegg.

"We have to get back up there!" gasped Sam. "There isn't another secret tunnel out from the bowling alley, is there, Captain?"

"No." Comet shook his head.

"Can we break the door down?" Sam suggested, looking at Romero, the strongest of the pirates.

The snippernaut started towards the door, but Pegg called him back. "Don't even try, you'll pulverise your pincers. That's Titanium wood – part wood, part steel."

Sam looked around in desperation. There was nothing in the alley except bowling pins, and the glimmer of starlight coming though the portholes.

Sam suddenly had an idea. As the bowling ball whizzed past he grabbed it and declared, "That's it – I've got it!"

"Good," said Comet. "Finally, my poor head is safe."

"No, not the ball – well, I've got that, too – but I've also got a plan!" said Sam. "Quick!" He ran down the bowling lane, staggering from side to side as the ship swayed, nearly falling over as he reached the small, round window.

"The porthole?" Pegg said, a rare smile splitting his face.

"But no one's small enough to fit through there," Comet spluttered.

"Except me!" Sam said. "See, Romero, being a space sprat is useful after all! If I can climb up to the deck I can open the door from the other side."

"But you could fall off into space!" Barney wrung his tentacles anxiously.

Sam looked around. "There's no other choice," he shrugged, trying not to sound too scared. "We have to get out of here. Romero, can you get the window open?"

Romero swung the window open and pulled it off its hinges. Sam looked at the pirates' worried faces and forced himself to smile. "Get ready," he said. "I'll make my way up to the deck, then sneak down here. When I open the door we're going to get Goldstar and *take our ship back*!"

Sam winced as the cold air rushed through the porthole. Outside there was nothing but deep dark empty space. If he slipped, he'd fall and float off forever, all the way down to Starry Jones's locker.

Mutiny!

He gulped. *Better not fall off then*, he thought to himself as he squeezed through the porthole.

Sam clung on to the outside of the ship, trying his best not to look down. The *Jolly Apollo* was made out Titanium wood, but it was old and rusty. The whole ship needed repairing – and washing! Space barnacles dotted the surface, and the gap between each wooden plank was furry with plants and scattered with shining meteor dust. For once Sam was pleased that the *Jolly Apollo* was an old space wreck. If the sides of the ship had been new, shiny and smooth he'd never have been able to climb up it.

Grabbing the nearest barnacle, Sam took a deep breath, and started to climb, carefully wedging his feet in the gaps between the planks, and pulling himself up bit by bit. *It's just like climbing up the mainsail,* he told himself with a gulp. *Just don't look down!*

The ship tilted wildly, and Sam's foot slipped, dangling out into deep space. There was a gasp from the porthole, where the pirates were

clustered, watching him.

Sam swung his leg back and wedged his foot into a gap between the boards, panting heavily.

The solar winds whistled around him, but Sam kept going. He was almost at the top when the ship jerked again. From the deck above he could hear smashes and crashes as things fell and shattered. Sam flattened himself against the side of the ship and held on tightly.

Just above his head, the ship's name was written in raised wooden letters. The "A" and both "l"s of "Apollo" had fallen off, so it actually spelt "*Jolly po o*". Sam reached up and grabbed the bottom of the J, then hauled himself up to balance on it. He peered on to the deck through a gap in the gunwhales. Goldstar was struggling with the sails and trying to steer at the same time. The main deck was scattered with ropes, grum tankards, dirty washing (including Barney's massive multi-legged pants) and barrels. Goldstar's black hair was sticking up crazily, and he was trying to shake a net off his peg leg while he pulled a rope with all his strength.

Taking his chance while Goldstar was distracted, Sam scrambled onboard, heaving himself up and sliding on to the deck belly-first. He lay silently for a minute, his heart pounding and his knees weak. He was so happy to be safely on the ship that he could have kissed the deck –

but there was no time for that. He still had to let the others out. If Goldstar saw him now he'd be back in the dungeon quicker than he could drink a glass of grum, and his climb would have been for nothing.

Sam crept across the deck towards the door down into the hold. But as he crept, the ship's wheel spun again and a barrel of grum smashed down next to him, bursting open and showering the deck with the foamy yellow liquid. Sam ducked behind another barrel as Goldstar glanced in the direction of the noise. Sam held his breath, but luckily at that moment the ship rocked violently in the other direction, flinging Goldstar on to his backside.

Sam scrambled to the doorway and half-fell down the steps. He raced forward and wrenched open the door to the bowling alley. With a great roar the crew flooded out, arming themselves with whatever they could find on their way. Comet led the charge, brandishing a mop and bucket like a sword and shield. Barney followed with a hoverpin in each tentacle, and Pegg and Legg with a bowling ball in each hand.

Sam grinned as he followed the pirates. But as he got back on deck he stopped short. The crew were huddled in a corner, looking at Goldstar, who had his laser-cutlass held against Captain Comet's throat.

"You'll have to get up earlier in the morning than that to fool old Goldstar, me lad," sneered the gold-caped pirate. "Now Comet here will pay the price – by walking the plank!"

Chapter Eleven

PLANK PERIL

Mutiny!

Comet edged out on the plank, still clutching the mop and bucket. Sam noticed that it was one of the buckets that had been used earlier for voting. His knees were knocking so hard that the end of the plank was starting to bounce up and down. Sam felt his throat go dry as he looked at his captain, hanging out over open space.

"You! Stabilise the ship," Goldstar snapped at Pegg and Legg. Then he turned to Sam. "My brother warned me to be on the lookout for you," he snarled. "He said you were slipperier than a Martian sand eel. I see he wasn't exaggerating. Unfortunately for you, you're not *quite* slippery enough."

"Stop right there, Goldstar," said Sam, summoning all his courage. "We're sick of you and we want our ship back!"

Goldstar laughed evilly.

"Oh, do you now? Well, I'm the elected captain of this here ship for the next three voyages, like it or not. Every single member of the crew voted for me, and now you're stuck with me." He gave

a wicked grin. "And as the captain, I sentence you and Patches here to take a one way trip down to Starry Jones's locker."

Everyone gasped as Goldstar waved his cutlass at the vast emptiness of space behind him.

"Time to say goodbye to the *Apollo* and hello to deep space," chortled Goldstar, prodding the cutlass in Comet's direction.

Sam was rooted to the spot in fear. But, just then, something caught his eye. There, on the deck among the dirty socks and rubbish, was a shiny pirate token... They hadn't all gone overboard after all!

"Goldstar!" he shouted.

"Wait your turn, small fry, it's Comet's go on the bouncy board first," Goldstar cackled.

"Oh, I don't think so – you don't have the authority," said Sam.

"What are you talking about, you stellar-slug?" barked Goldstar. "I'm the captain!"

"Ah, but you're not!" Sam grinned. "To be the new captain the vote has to be unanimous, which means all crew members have to vote for you. If the existing captain gets one vote, he stays where he is."

"Yeah, so what?" Goldstar replied.

Sam leaped into the pile of old socks strewn across the deck. He grabbed the shining token and held it up. "I haven't voted!" Sam declared. "You might have tempted the rest of the crew with endless grum and supernova floss, but not me. I'm a crew member on this ship and I'm going to vote now."

He flipped the token through the air. Everyone watched as it flew, glinting in the light as it spun past Goldstar, out over the edge of the ship and into Comet's bucket with a satisfying clink. "I vote for Captain Comet!"

Comet looked so relieved that Sam was worried he might faint.

He sank down on to the plank and hugged it with his arms and legs.

Goldstar stared at Sam furiously. "You devious dirt devil! You pugnacious pug-rat! You spit-mouthed slime toad!" He paused for breath, then grinned like a madman as he pulled something out of his pocket. Sam gasped as he saw the scrap of spacesuit material.

"If I'm not getting to Planet X," Goldstar laughed, "then *nobody* is."

Cackling maniacally, he grabbed the map in both hands and tried to rip it in half. But the spacesuit material was too tough. Sam rushed forwards as Goldstar twisted and pulled the precious fabric. "Say goodbye to your parents, you irritating little space slug," Goldstar crowed. "And say goodbye to Planet… ERRRFFFF!"

From behind, Captain Comet slammed his bucket down on top of Goldstar's head, wedging it fast.

Goldstar dropped the map, and Sam dived forward to pick it up. His heart thudded frantically as he smoothed it out, but the strong spacesuit material wasn't damaged. Sam heaved a huge sigh of relief and tucked the map safely into his pocket.

Goldstar pulled off the bucket, and Comet's captain's hat went flying across the deck. Comet grabbed hold of one edge of Goldstar's cape.

"I think we should take Goldstar for a spin, don't you?" he yelled.

With the rest of the crew cheering, he gave the cape a huge tug which sent Goldstar spinning across the deck. He came to a halt at the top of the stairs that led down to the bowling deck. Comet sauntered across the deck and with a well-aimed swipe of his mop, smacked Goldstar square on the backside. The blow sent Goldstar tumbling down the stairs.

Comet craned his neck to listen to the thumps and bumps of Goldstar's progress down the stairs. With a bash and a groan, Goldstar came to a halt at the bottom and Comet gave a quick nod of approval.

"Ah, it's good to be back, Sam," said the captain as he looked out from the deck rail at the colourful spread of galaxies in front of them.

"I think we all agree on that one, Captain," said Sam. "Look behind you."

Comet turned round and there assembled on the main deck was the entire crew. Pegg and Legg stepped forward from the crowd, shuffling their feet and looking embarrassed.

...alf of the crew, we'd like to say a few
... said Legg. "Firstly, we'd like to say sorry
for ...oting for Goldstar. It just sounded like a lot
of fun; you know, the supernova floss…"

"And the grum…" shouted someone.

"And the funfairs…" shouted someone else.

"Yes, yes, I get the idea," said Comet snappily.

"And Goldstar *sounded* like he would be such
a good captain…" Legg continued.

"Aye, and you've been rubbish!" said Pegg.
"Most of the time we're lost and we've never
found any treasure, ever. Not even by accident."

"OK, OK," said Comet. "This must be the
worst apology in space pirate history."

"But even saying all that, we're glad you're
back," Pegg finished. "You and the *Jolly Apollo*
go together like…"

"Bowling balls and hoverpins," shouted
Vulpus.

"Pirates and grum," shouted Jonjarama.

"Scab-beetle stew and slime-moss sandwiches,"
said Barney.

"Aye, like all of those – though perhaps not the last one – but you know what we mean," said Legg.

"So we think you need this back," said Sam. He picked up Comet's captain's hat from the deck and handed it to him. It was a bit bent and battered, but Comet didn't seem to mind. He took a handkerchief from his pocket and dabbed his eyes, even the ones with eyepatches on.

"Why, thank you, me hearties," he said, carefully placing the hat back on his head. "And I think we've all learned something from this. You probably more than me, I'd say, but it's good to be back all the same."

Sam rolled his eyes – the old Comet was definitely back. A sudden banging from the bowling alley made him jump. "But what are we going to do with Goldstar?" he asked.

"Oh, I've got a plan for Goldstar – *and* his brother," said Comet with a smile. "You can be sure about that. Just leave that to *Captain* Joseph Hercules Invictus Comet!"

Chapter Twelve

COMET'S REVENGE

Mutiny!

The crew members were spread in a semi-circle on the main deck, gathered round a large holoscreen that was hooked up to the ship's telescope. They were perched on barrels, or sitting cross-legged on the floor, all keenly awaiting the entertainment that was about to come. They chatted and joked and clinked their tankards of grum together. It wasn't often that you could take anything for granted on board the *Jolly Apollo*, but this time everyone was pretty sure it was going to be brilliant.

"I think I see it," said Vulpus, spotting the tiny dot on the holoscreen.

The dot grew larger and as it increased in size it took on a form. Slowly the shape became clearer – it was Black-Hole Beard's ship, *Gravity's Revenge*. Everyone booed and hissed as it approached. Sam grinned – this was by far the best way to see the *Revenge*: from a very safe distance. Bit by bit the menacing form began to fill the screen; the hull bristling with laser cannons, the midnight-black sails billowing in the solar winds.

"Can you zoom in any closer?" asked Comet. "I'd hate to miss anything!"

There were conspiratorial chuckles from the crew. Sam fiddled with the dial on the telescope in front of him. The image on the holoscreen went blurry briefly, then focused in on the approaching ship, showing what was happening on the main deck of the *Revenge*. The enormous first-mate, Yarr, was striding about directing Black-Hole Beard's crew, who leaped around the ship in an impressive display of almost robotic efficiency. One-Hand Luke, a particularly fearsome-looking crew member, was using his hydraulic hook to winch in the sails. Much as the *Apollo*'s crew were looking forward to what was going to happen, they were still intimidated by how good the *Revenge*'s crew were. The door to the Captain's cabin opened.

"Ah, the main attraction," said Comet.

The crew giggled.

"And don't he look fancy!" said Pegg.

Much to the *Apollo* crew's amusement, Black-Hole Beard did indeed look very fancy.

Black-Hole Beard, scourge of the galaxies, terror of the interstellar regions, voted meanest pirate alive for the last twelve years running, was dressed in what looked like a pirate outfit designed by the girliest girl in the Universe – one with an addiction to lace.

"That's the dress uniform of a fleet admiral," Comet explained longingly.

"It's very … flouncy!" Sam giggled.

There were more ruffles on the sleeves than on anything Sam had ever seen before. The formal frock coat rippled to the floor and pooled on to the deck in a long train. Even Black-Hole Beard's wiry black beard was neatly combed and plaited, the ends tied in a bow. He looked like a Yillapian Gorilla squeezed into a dress.

"He's wearing *knickerbockers*!" shouted Legg in hysterical disbelief.

The crew exploded in laughter as Black-Hole Beard strutted around his deck in a pair of frilly pantaloons that even he couldn't make look tough. He stopped and adjusted the pale, baby-blue tricorn hat with lace edging and smiled happily.

"Bless his frilly pants, he looks so pleased with himself," said Comet, taking a sip of grum.

"Ain't he going to be disappointed?" laughed Pegg.

"It's just a pity we haven't got any sound," said Sam. "I wish I could hear what he's saying."

Gravity's Revenge was fast approaching the asteroid where it was meant to meet the *Jolly Apollo*. Things were getting so exciting that Jonjarama let out a squeaky little trump. On screen, confusion flashed over Black-Hole Beard's face as he caught sight of the asteroid.

"There he blows!" Pegg crowed as Black-Hole Beard's face turned redder and redder.

"Bring up the asteroid please, Sam," said Comet.

"Aye, aye, Captain," Sam replied.

He swivelled the telescope towards the asteroid

that they were currently speeding away from. On it cowered Goldstar. Black-Hole Beard's younger brother was marooned there wearing only his gold cape, his pants and a look of extreme embarrassment. As he stared at his big brother he mouthed the word, "Sorry".

Sam swivelled the telescope back so that it focused on the *Revenge*. As the delighted crew watched, Black-Hole Beard snatched the baby-blue admiral's hat from his head and screwed it into a tight ball. He let out a bellow of rage, which Sam could have sworn he heard even though they were twenty space-knots away.

The crew rolled round the deck, roaring with laughter. Sam laughed until he cried, and his stomach ached more than it had after he'd had second helpings of Barney's Stovacian Surprise Stew.

Finally Captain Comet wiped tears from under his eyepatches and flicked off the screen, where Black-Hole Beard was jumping up and down and hitting his brother with his ruined hat.

"Right-ho me hearties, that's enough," said Comet, beaming at his crew. "All we're going to get now is Captain Fancy Pants prancing around in his frilly knickers, and frankly, I'm in too good a mood to see that hairy old party-pooper! Piole, would you be so kind as to find somewhere to store our treasure?"

Comet passed over Goldstar's solid gold bowling ball.

"Best give the old treasure chest a clean first," Comet continued. "It'll be a bit dusty, no doubt."

Sam glanced round the crew and felt a surge of happiness. "What next, Captain?" he asked.

"It's no good hanging around." Comet patted his hat as if to check it was still there, then nodded to his first mate. "Mr Pegg and Mr Legg, please set the wheel hard to starboard and plot a new course. We've still got a planet to find. The *Jolly Apollo* is back on its way to Planet X!"

"Aye, aye, Cap'n," both of the first mate's heads replied.

"But first a toast," said Comet, rising to

his feet. "To Planet X and success!"

"To Planet X and success!" the crew cheered and each took a long drink of grum.

"Captain, with your permission I'd like to make a toast, too," said Sam. He raised his glass high in the air.

"To Captain Comet and the best crew in the entire Universe! The *Jolly Apollo*!"

"To adventures and excitement!" Barney added as they clinked their grum glasses.

"And to Black-Hole Beard's frilly pants!" Sam laughed.

"Hear, hear!" everyone shouted. "Hear, hear!"

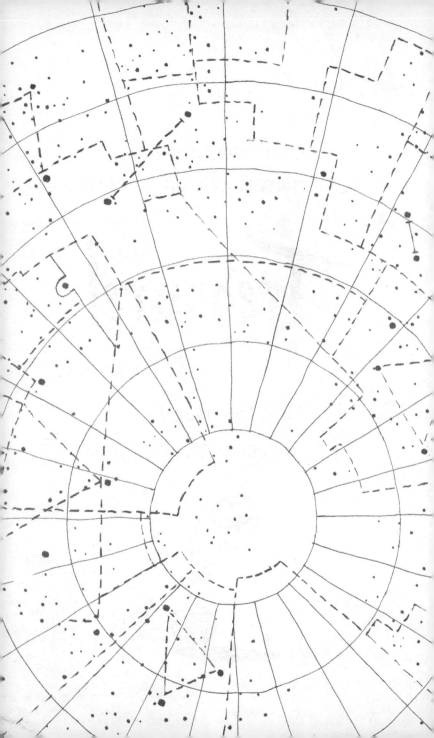

Can't wait for the
next intergalactic adventure?

Turn the page for
a sneaky peek!

Chapter One

BREAKFAST AND WORMHOLES

Treasure!

Samson Starbuck leaned on the rail that ran around the crow's nest of the pirate spaceship, the *Jolly Apollo*, and looked at the endless stretch of the Universe around him. The deep black of space was scattered with colourful clouds of gas, the short, bright tail of a slow moving purple comet and countless pinpricks of light. Sam knew that each one of those lights was a star, and each of those stars could be surrounded by planets. And on one of those planets, his parents were space-shipwrecked and waiting to be rescued.

Sam turned his attention to the tattered piece of cloth in his hand. It was a rough map that his mum had managed to draw on a scrap of spacesuit material and send to Sam in their ship's homing beacon. It showed the way to the planet where his parents' spaceship had crashed while they'd been scouring the galaxies for new forms of plant life.

Sam's only hope of rescuing his parents had been to stowaway on a space pirate ship. Luckily, they had landed on the fabled Planet X, which space-pirate myth claimed was a famous treasure

planet made of solid gold, with islands of rubies. When the pirates found out he had a map to Planet X, they were happy to let Sam join the crew.

As Sam had discovered, choosing the *Apollo* was both the best *and* worst decision he could have made. The crew were terrible at being pirates: they were always getting lost, they never found any treasure, they argued with each other and the food on board was terrible. However they were also kind-hearted, loved a good space-shanty, enjoyed a game of ten-pin bowling (all pirate ships had at least one bowling alley on board), and always looked out for each other – including Sam, who was now the cabin boy.

"Korraaaackkkkkk! Korraaaackkkkkk!"

A terrible sound battered the silence of Sam's lookout post.

"Korraaaackkkkkk! Korraaaackkkkkk!"

The deafening screech rattled around the *Apollo* again. Sam groaned. The noise was coming from a Pgtargan cockerel, the noisiest type of bird in the tri-galaxy network. Captain

Treasure!

Comet had bought it at the last space port. He reckoned the crew needed something to get them up in the mornings, which was probably true, but the cockerel had swiftly become the least popular thing on board the ship. In fact, it was probably the least popular thing to ever have been on any Space Pirate ship, and that was saying something. Even from the top of the main mast Sam could hear the curses of his shipmates.

But it wasn't the only noise Sam could hear – there was also the unmistakable sound of someone climbing the rigging to the crow's nest. And by the awful smell wafting upwards it had to be Barney, the ship's cook, with breakfast. A large tentacle curled over the edge of the rail and moments later Barney hauled himself up next to Sam. It was a bit of a tight squeeze in the crow's nest as Barney was a huge multi-tentacled Kraken. He looked truly terrifying…